Cinderella— WITH DOGS!

LINDA BAILEY

illustrated by
FREYA HARTAS

 Nancy Paulsen Books

NANCY PAULSEN BOOKS

An imprint of Penguin Random House LLC, New York

First published in the United States of America by Nancy Paulsen Books,
an imprint of Penguin Random House LLC, 2023

Text copyright © 2023 by Linda Bailey
Illustrations copyright © 2023 by Freya Hartas

Visit us online at penguinrandomhouse.com.

Library of Congress Cataloging-in-Publication Data is available.

Manufactured in China

ISBN 9781984813824

1 3 5 7 9 10 8 6 4 2

TOPL

Edited by Nancy Paulsen | Art directed and designed by Marikka Tamura
Text set in Bodoni Egyptian Pro
The illustrations for this book were made digitally using the program Clip Studio.

Poor Cinderella, lonely and sad, was sweeping the ashes from the fireplace. Everyone else had gone off to the ball to dance. *She* had to stay home—and work!

Poor Cinderella never went anywhere. She never had a single bit of fun.

Ever!

"If only I had a fairy godmother," she said.

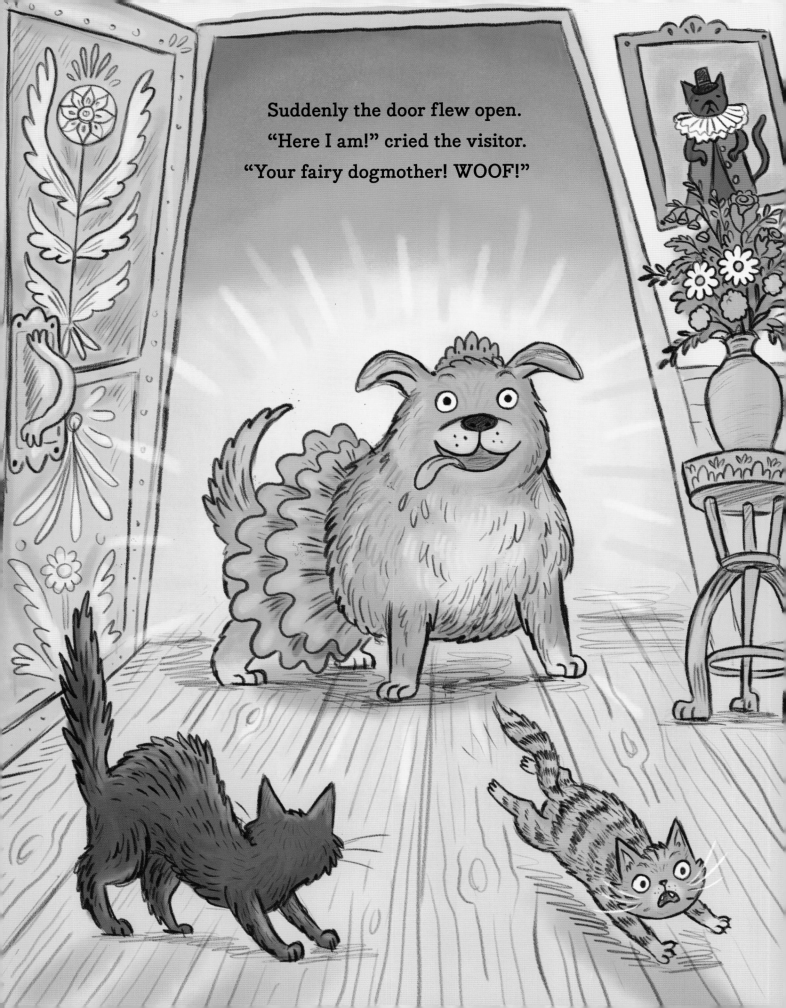

Suddenly the door flew open.
"Here I am!" cried the visitor.
"Your fairy dogmother! WOOF!"

Cinderella gasped. "Did you say . . . *dog*mother?"

"I did indeed," said the visitor.

"Oh dear," said Cinderella. "I'm supposed to have a fairy *godmother*. Not a *dogmother*."

The dog hung her head. "You mean . . . you don't want me?"

Cinderella knew how it felt to be unwanted.
She also happened to be very fond of dogs.
"I suppose we could give it a try," she said.
"Oh good!" said the dog. "Because *you* need
some cheering up. Let's chase SQUIRRELS!"

"Squirrels?" asked Cinderella. But she followed the dog outside. Soon they were chasing squirrels all over the lawn.

Cinderella was surprised to find that she *did* feel more cheerful. It was the first time she'd been outside in weeks!

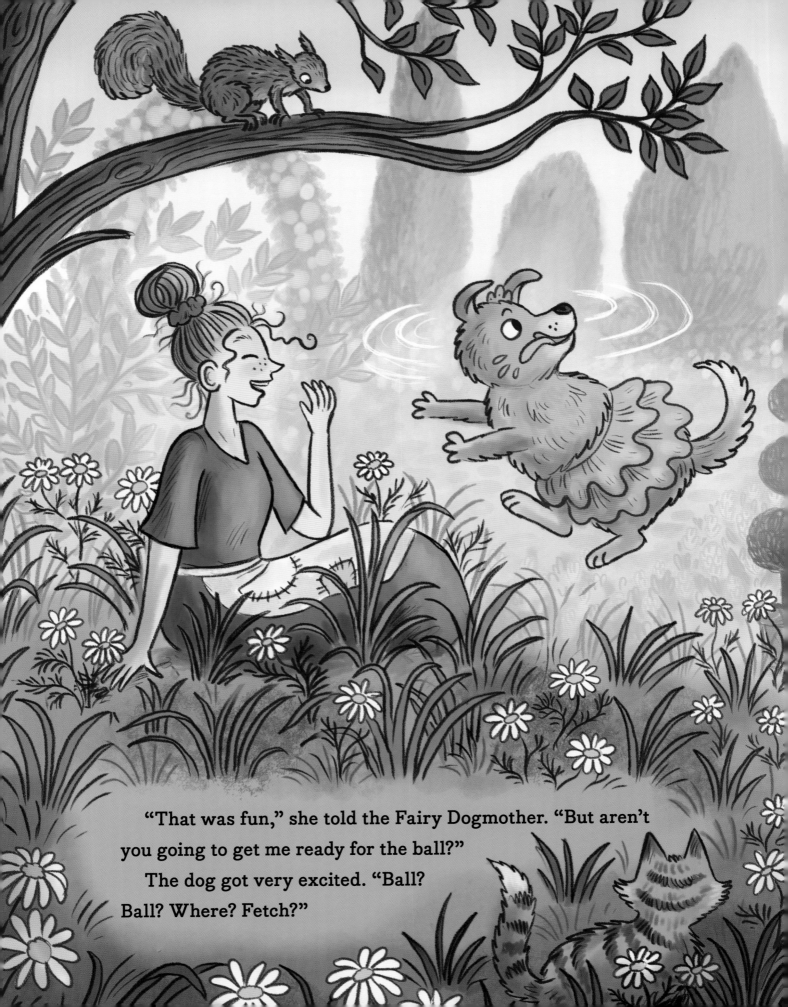

"That was fun," she told the Fairy Dogmother. "But aren't
you going to get me ready for the ball?"
The dog got very excited. "Ball?
Ball? Where? Fetch?"

"Not *that* kind of ball," said Cinderella. "It's the fancy kind where you dance. You're supposed to dress me up."

"I am?" said the dog. "Well, why didn't you say so?"

She reached into her tutu, pulled out a magic wand, and waved it at Cinderella. "WOOF! POOF!"

"Holey moley," said Cinderella. "What's *this*? Looks like an old dog blanket."

"That's exactly what it is!" said the Fairy Dogmother. "Doesn't it smell divine?"

Cinderella gave it a sniff. It wasn't a *regular* ball gown, but it was cozy. And she *did* love the fleecy bits. So she smiled.

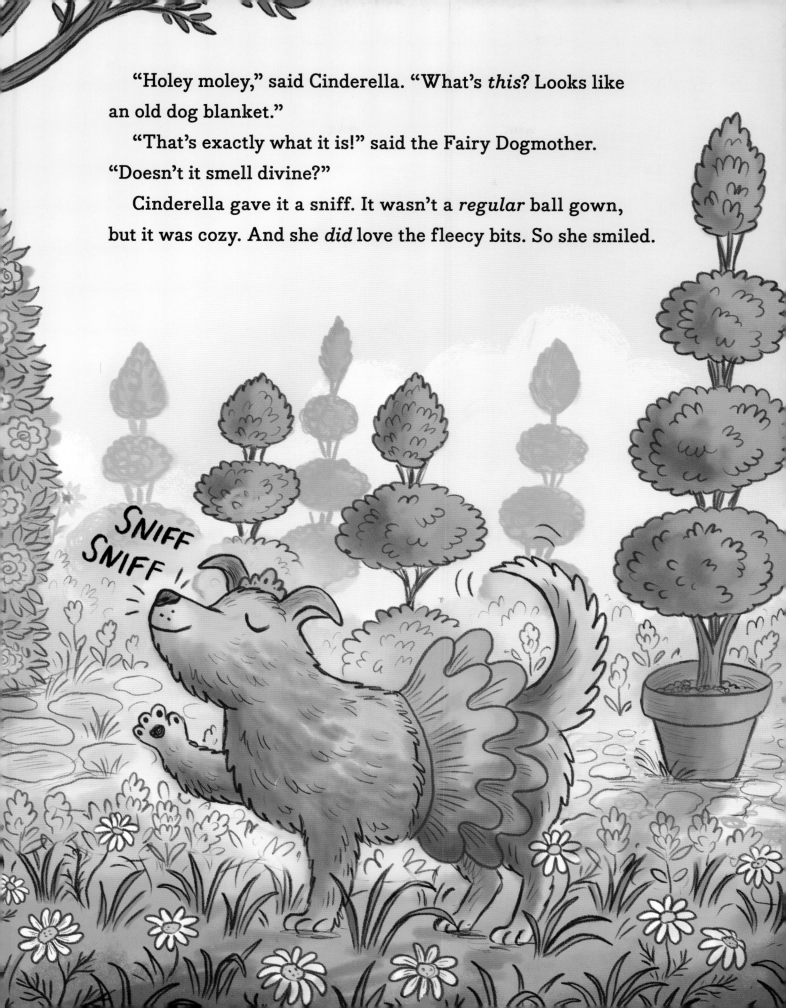

SNIFF
SNIFF

"Perfect!" the Fairy Dogmother said. "Now your hair."
She waved her wand again. "WOOF! POOF!"

Cinderella ran to a mirror.
"Oh my goodness," she said.
"I look like a poodle!"
"You do!" cried the dog.
"I'm so jealous."

"What about shoes?" asked Cinderella.

"Overrated," said the Fairy Dogmother. "Somebody put booties on *me* once. They just fall right off."

Cinderella shook her head. "I can't go to a ball barefoot."

"Very well," said the dog, reaching into her tutu again. "I still have a couple of those booties."

"You look fabulous!" said the Fairy Dogmother. "Time to go!"
"Go?" Cinderella asked. "Aren't you supposed to make me
a fancy carriage? With horses and footmen?"

"I suppose I could," said the dog. "But it's so much more fun to RUN! Wouldn't you like a good run? And a grand old howl on the way?"

As it so happened,
Cinderella *was* very fond of running.
Chasing the squirrels had reminded her.

She had never tried howling before.
But there was a full moon that night,
and when the Fairy Dogmother burst
into howls, it seemed natural for
Cinderella to join in.

AWOOOOOOO

AWOO

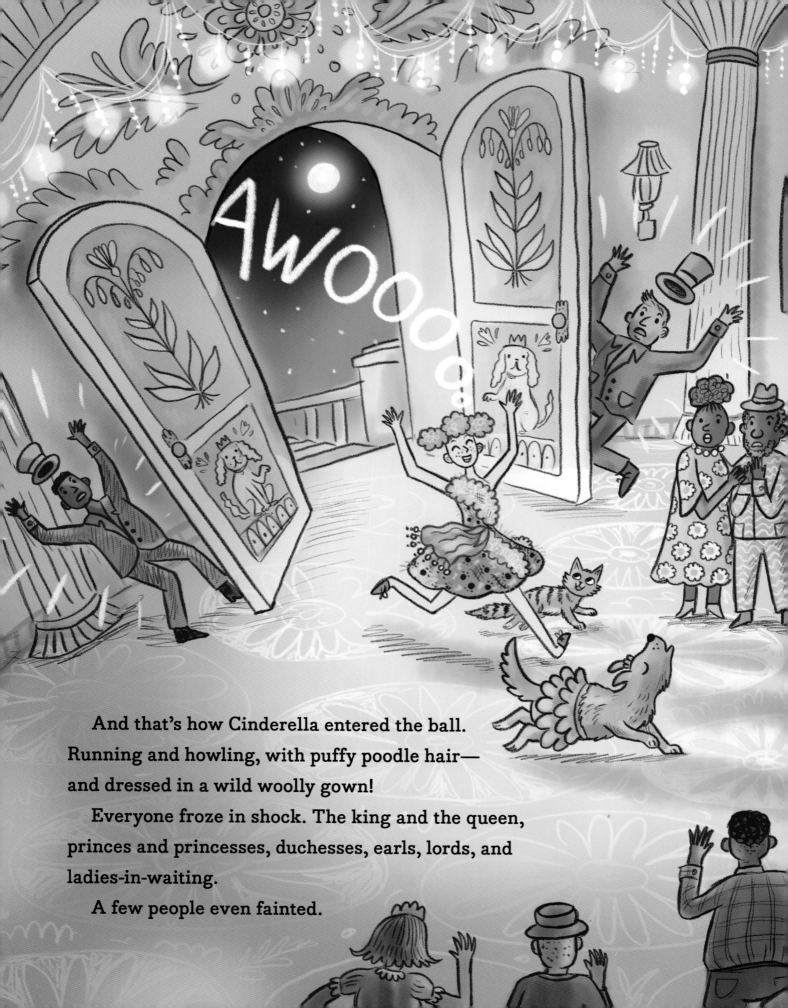

Awoooo...

And that's how Cinderella entered the ball.
Running and howling, with puffy poodle hair—
and dressed in a wild woolly gown!

Everyone froze in shock. The king and the queen,
princes and princesses, duchesses, earls, lords, and
ladies-in-waiting.

A few people even fainted.

But the king and the queen didn't faint. Nor did the prince or the princess. That's because the royal family *loved* dogs. They had dozens of dogs! They couldn't get enough of them!

And at that very moment, the royal dogs ran in. Cinderella dropped to the floor and gave each dog a hug.

"She's a marvel!" said the king.
"I adore her!" said the queen.
"Love the hair!" said the princess.
"Yowzers!" cried the prince. "She's AMAZING!"

He asked her to dance. She said yes.
Around and around they danced all evening,
and the dogs danced too.
The prince was enchanted!

But when the ball ended, they had to say goodbye—
and that's when one of Cinderella's booties fell off.

"Look!" said the prince as he picked it up.
"I will keep this precious slipper so that I can
find you again."

Cinderella laughed. "Don't worry," she said.
"Your dogs will find me anywhere!"

She was right. The very next day, the dogs tracked her down.
And of course, the bootie fit her foot. And of course, the prince
asked her to marry him.

"Well, thanks," said Cinderella. "But I hardly know you! Why don't we have some fun together instead? Have you ever chased SQUIRRELS?"

And that's just what they did!